15
FIREFIGHTER
PeneLope
SECRET AGENT
PeneLope
FAIRY
PeneLope

PENNY
and

PENELOPE

WRITTEN BY DAN RICHARDS
ILLUSTRATED BY CLAIRE ALMON

Imprint
MAKE YOUR MARK
NEW YORK

I'm so glad you
could come over!

Isn't it the most perfect room ever? Wait till you see what I have.

Princess

This is my Princess Penelope doll.
She's wearing her eggshell-blue evening gown
with real glass slippers and a diamond tiara.

Isn't she beautiful?

Cool. I have
a Penny doll, too.

Is that a motorcycle jacket
she's wearing?

Yeah, isn't it awesome?

Penny's a secret agent
on the lookout
for danger.

Um . . . Let's have a tea party.
Penny can be a princess visiting from a faraway kingdom.

Penny isn't a princess.

Well, Penelope *is* a princess.

Let's ride our ponies through the countryside.
The clover is lovely this time of year.

Penny doesn't have a pony.
She has a turbocharged racing bike with a real, working headlight.

Perhaps we should wave to
our adoring subjects.

Look out!
There's a crocodile in the moat!

The villagers are in danger!
SPLASH!!!
Oh dear, you're going to need a soak in a warm bubble bath.
No time.

It's getting dark and there's a wolf on the prowl.

There are no wolves in my kingdom!

Worse! It's a *werewolf*!

We have to get out of here!

But princesses only ride ponies!

There are no ponies out here—hang on tight!

Look, my dress is torn. And my glass slipper is gone.
I'm very upset. Was there really a werewolf in the forest?

Not anymore. It's crept inside your private tower.

What do we do?

There's only one thing left that we can do.
Stay quiet and hope the pony is enough . . .

Enough what?

Enough of a meal.

THE WEREWOLF IS
NOT EATING MY PONY!

Look, you're just a princess,
and I'm just a secret agent
who's in over her head.

Just a princess?

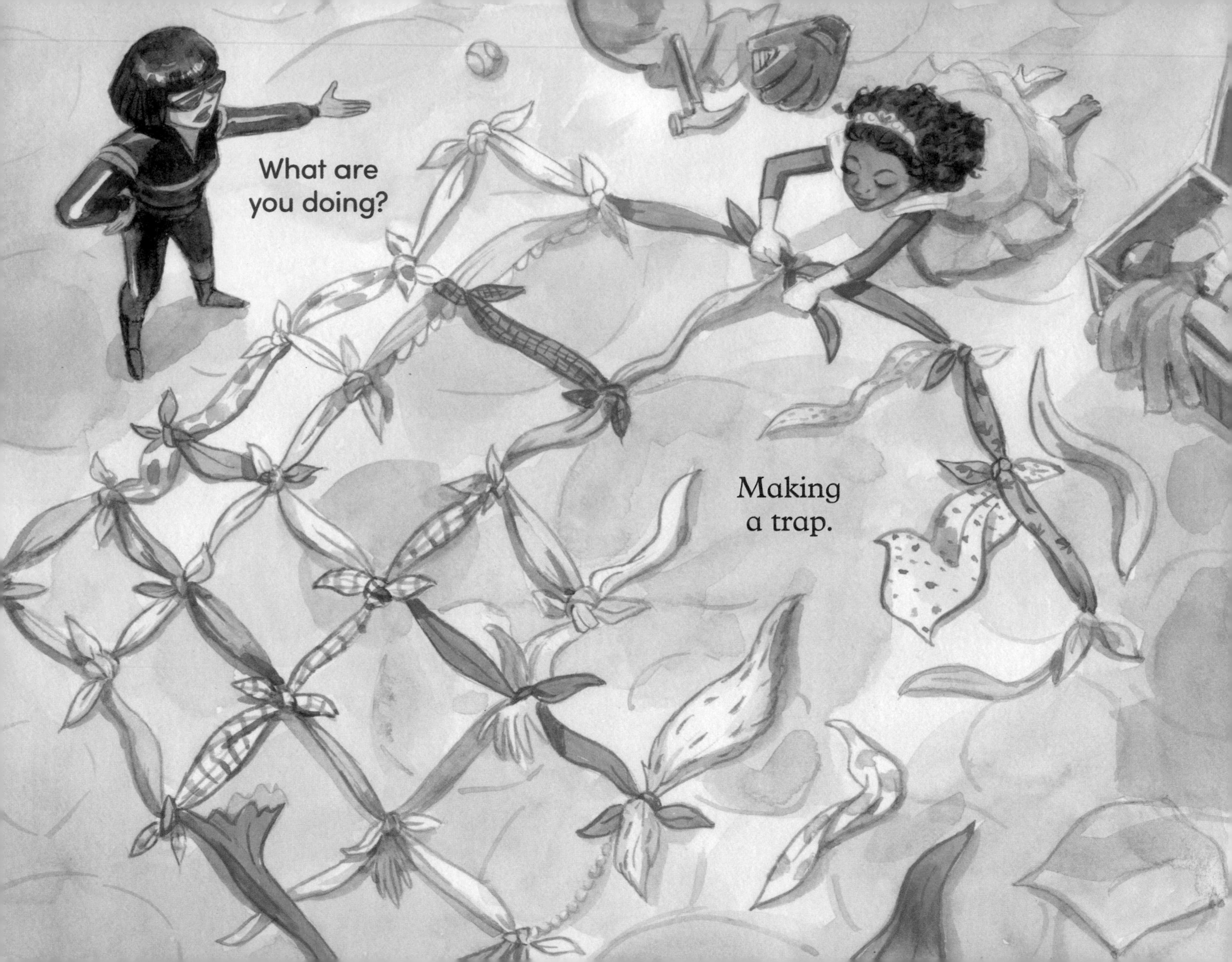

What are
you doing?

Making
a trap.

I didn't know you could do that.

Princesses are *very* resourceful.

I know how to tie a square knot.

Then you can help.

Now all we need is bait.

Everyone knows that werewolves *love* princesses.

They do?

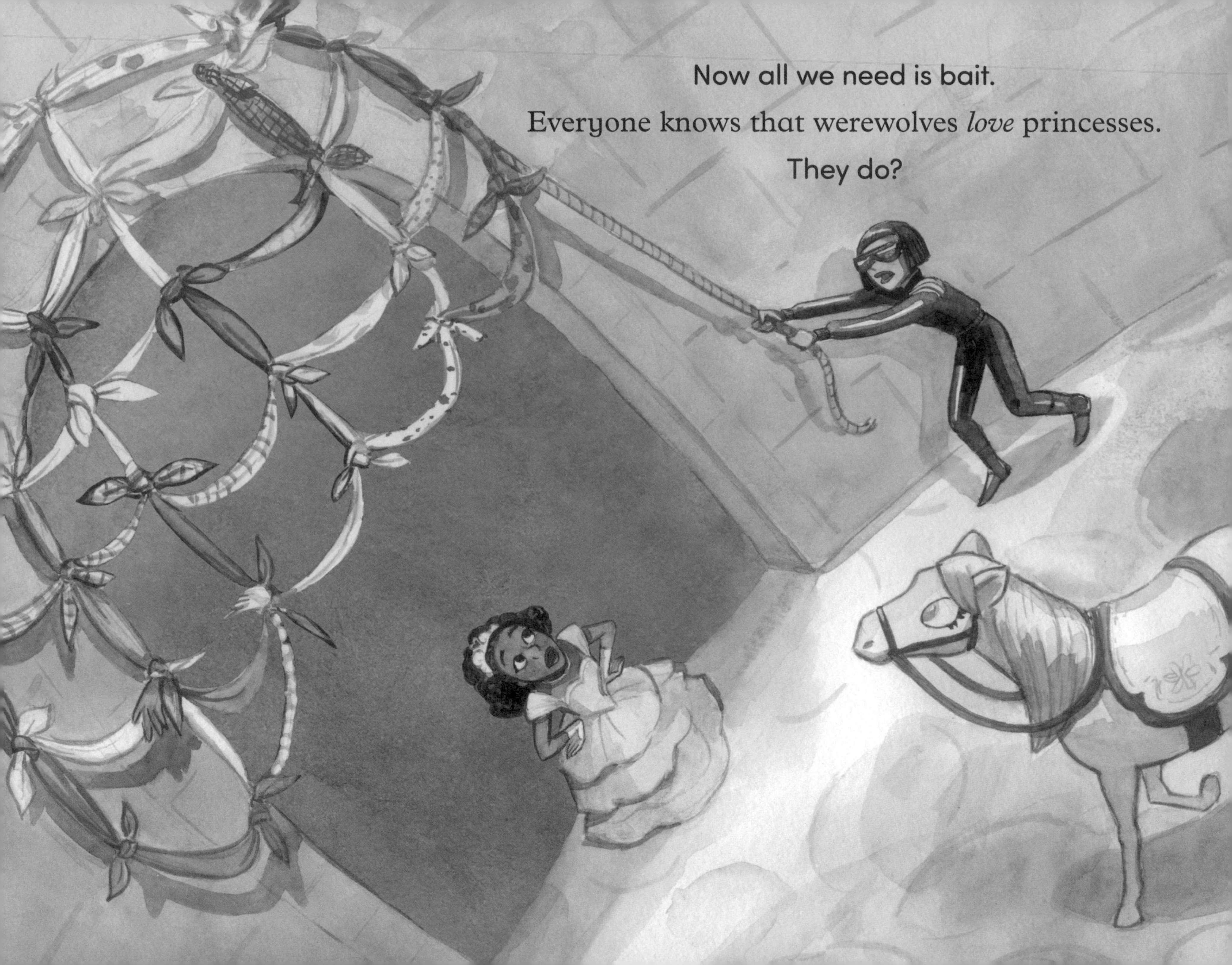

Of course. Wait here while I ride my pony into the hallway and lure it into the trap.

Okay, but your pony might get spooked. Better take my bike.

Excuse me, werewolf? Here I am. Come and get me.

I don't see anything.

Wolfy, wolfy,
here I am.
Come and get
me if you can.
NOW!

Try singing. Werewolves are drawn to singing.

Gotcha!

We did it!

I never knew capturing werewolves could be so much fun.
You were right. Penny really *is* a secret agent.

And Penelope really *is* a princess.

Maybe tomorrow we can go
on another adventure.

Wait!
Cyborg Penelope
is in trouble!

Uh-oh. Looks like someone needs our help now!

For Angela, Malia, and Sue. —D.R.

For my nieces and nephew. —C.A.

[Imprint]
A part of Macmillan Publishing Group, LLC
175 Fifth Avenue, New York, NY 10010

ABOUT THIS BOOK
The art in this book was created with watercolor.
The text was set in Plantin MT and Sofia Pro Soft.
The book was edited by Nicole Otto and Rhoda Belleza,
and designed by Natalie C. Sousa.
The production was supervised by Raymond Ernesto Colón,
and the production editor was Dawn Ryan.

PENNY AND PENELOPE. Text copyright © 2019 by Dan Richards.
Illustrations copyright © 2019 by Imprint. All rights reserved. Printed
in China by Hung Hing Off-set Printing Co. Ltd., Heshan City,
Guangdong Province.

Library of Congress Control Number: 2018955725

ISBN 978-1-250-15607-5

Our books may be purchased in bulk for promotional, educational,
or business use. Please contact your local bookseller or the Macmillan
Corporate and Premium Sales Department at (800) 221-7945 ext. 5442
or by email at MacmillanSpecialMarkets@macmillan.com.

Illustrations by Claire Almon
Imprint logo designed by Amanda Spielman

First edition, 2019

10 9 8 7 6 5 4 3 2 1

mackids.com

The unlawful possessor of this book will be
tracked down by a team of princesses,
secret agents, cyborgs, firefighters,
punk rockers, and vengeful fairies.
Oh, and a werewolf . . .
and alligator . . .
and a pony.